W9-AET-499

THE HUNCHBACK OF NOTRE DAME

VICTOR MARIE HUGO

SADDLEBACK
EDUCATIONAL PUBLISHING

Saddleback's *Illustrated Classics*™

SADDLEBACK
EDUCATIONAL PUBLISHING
www.sdlback.com

© 2006 by Saddleback Educational Publishing
All rights reserved. No part of this book may be reproduced in any form or by any means, electronic or mechanical, including photocopying, recording, scanning, or by any information storage and retrieval system, without the written permission of the publisher.

ISBN-13: 978-1-56254-908-4
ISBN-10: 1-56254-908-1
eBook: 978-1-60291-153-6

Printed in Guangzhou, China
1109/11-68-09

15 14 13 12 11 10 09 2 3 4 5 6 7 8

Welcome to
Saddleback's *Illustrated Classics*™

We are proud to welcome you to Saddleback's *Illustrated Classics*™. Saddleback's *Illustrated Classics*™ was designed specifically for the classroom to introduce readers to many of the great classics in literature. Each text, written and adapted by teachers and researchers, has been edited using the Dale-Chall vocabulary system. In addition, much time and effort has been spent to ensure that these high-interest stories retain all of the excitement, intrigue, and adventure of the original books.

With these graphically *Illustrated Classics*™ , you learn what happens in the story in a number of different ways. One way is by reading the words a character says. Another way is by looking at the drawings of the character. The artist can tell you what kind of person a character is and what he or she is thinking or feeling.

This series will help you to develop confidence and a sense of accomplishment as you finish each novel. The stories in Saddleback's *Illustrated Classics*™ are fun to read. And remember, fun motivates!

Overview

Everyone deserves to read the best literature our language has to offer. Saddleback's *Illustrated Classics*™ was designed to acquaint readers with the most famous stories from the world's greatest authors, while teaching essential skills. You will learn how to:

• Establish a purpose for reading
• Use prior knowledge
• Evaluate your reading
• Listen to the language as it is written
• Extend literary and language appreciation through discussion and
  writing activities

Reading is one of the most important skills you will ever learn. It provides the key to all kinds of information. By reading the *Illustrated Classics*™ , you will develop confidence and the self-satisfaction that comes from accomplishment— a solid foundation for any reader.

Step-By-Step

The following is a simple guide to using and enjoying each of your *Illustrated Classics*™ . To maximize your use of the learning activities provided, we suggest that you follow these steps:

1. ***Listen!*** We suggest that you listen to the read-along. (At this time, please ignore the beeps.) You will enjoy this wonderfully dramatized presentation.

2. ***Pre-reading Activities.*** After listening to the audio presentation, the pre-reading activities in the Activity Book prepare you for reading the story by setting the scene, introducing more difficult vocabulary words, and providing some short exercises.

3. ***Reading Activities.*** Now turn to the "While you are reading" portion of the Activity Book, which directs you to make a list of story-related facts. Read-along while listening to the audio presentation. (This time pay attention to the beeps, as they indicate when each page should be turned.)

4. ***Post-reading Activities.*** You have successfully read the story and listened to the audio presentation. Now answer the multiple-choice questions and other activities in the Activity Book.

Remember,

"Today's readers are tomorrow's leaders."

Victor Hugo

Victor Hugo, a French poet and novelist, was born in 1802. His life can be divided into seven periods: his Napoleonic childhood, his infant-prodigy period in Paris, his royalist period, the three turbulent years of the romantic crusade, the fifteen successful years under Louis Philippe, his political period, and his eighteen years of exile.

Hugo's ambition to become a writer began at the age of fourteen. From then on he wrote verses, odes, satires, acrostics, riddles, epics, and madrigals. At the age of twenty-two he published his first volume of poetry.

During his fifteen years of success he published one of his greatest works, *The Hunchback of Notre Dame*. Some of Hugo's immortal characters, Quasimodo, La Esmeralda, Phoebus, and Dom Frollo, will live on forever. With this work he acquired great popularity among all classes and is considered one of the most noted writers in French literature. He continued to write and completed another timeless world classic, *Les Miserables*, in 1861.

Because of his political activities, Hugo was forced to leave France in 1850. But with the great succes of *The Hunchback of Notre Dame* and *Les Miserables*, when Hugo died in 1885, all of France seemed to be in mourning.

Saddleback's *Illustrated Classics*™

THE HUNCHBACK OF NOTRE DAME

VICTOR MARIE HUGO

THE MAIN CHARACTERS

Gringoire

La Esmeralda

Quasimodo

Dom Frollo

Phoebus

A great ringing of bells greeted the double holiday of January 6, 1482, Epiphany and the Festival of Fools. In Paris it was to be celebrated with fireworks in the Place de Greve, and a play performed at the Palace of Justice.

This was announced in public places, with the sounding of a trumpet, by the major's officers in their fine uniforms.

At noon there was to be a play and also the arrival of the high officials. But both were late, and the crowd became restless. Students, soldiers, tradesmen, beggars, the crowd filled the Palace of Justice.

The play! The play!

The play, or we'll hang the Palace Bailiff!

A frightened actor dressed as a god appeared.

As soon as the Cardinal arrives, we shall begin.

The crowd booed angrily. A tall, fair young man stepped forward.

Start now!

Down with Jupiter!

Down with the Cardinal!

Jupiter—begin at once! I will explain to the Cardinal.

As the play began, a girl in the front row spoke to the young man.

I wrote it myself!

You did?

Will this be a very fine play?

Certainly!

Yes! I am Pierre Gringoire!

As the play continued, a ragged beggar climbed up to a ledge below the balcony and seated himself.

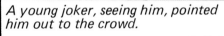
A young joker, seeing him, pointed him out to the crowd.

Look at the beggar there!

Speak kindly of me, if you please!

The actors stopped. Every head turned. Gringoire was upset.

The play went on again. The audience listened patiently. All at once the door of the balcony was thrown open.

Why the devil did you stop? Go on! Go on!

His Eminence the Cardinal!

Every head turned toward the Cardinal. Again the unlucky play was cut short.

The play! Go on with the play!

But the Cardinal was followed by a long line of famous guests: ambassadors from Austria, high officials from Flanders, and finally....

Jacques Coppenole of Ghent!

The crowd found the
noble guests more
interesting than the play.
Every eye was on the
balcony. Gringoire lost
hope.

At last everyone had arrived. The actors
went on. Suddenly Master Coppenole
rose from his seat.

Gentlemen, is
this what you
call a play? It
is not one bit
funny! They
promised I
should see the
election of a
Pope of Fools.

We have our
Pope of Fools
at Ghent, too.
But the way
we do it is
this. . . .

We collect a crowd;
then everyone
who wants to, puts
his head through
a hole and grins
at the crowd. The
ugliest face is
chosen Pope.

Shall we
choose your
Pope that way?

Yes!

Good!

Fine!

Only when he was brought out in front of the curtain was it discovered that the face was his real face.

It is Quasimodo, the bell ringer!

It is the hunchback of Notre Dame!

You are the finest piece of ugliness I ever saw!

He is deaf, sir.

Deaf! Can he speak?

He can talk when he likes. He became deaf from ringing the bells.

A paper crown and a poor robe were placed on him and he was carried on the shoulders of twelve men.

There was a look of hateful pride on his face as he saw beneath him, the heads of those straight, well-shaped men.

The parade moved off through the streets. Gringoire felt a hope of finishing his play.

Good! We shall get rid of those troublemakers.

Unluckily, the crowd rushed after them. In a moment the great hall was nearly empty.

Well, their number is small, but they are a good audience!

All at once a shout came from a young man in a window.

Those who were left in the hall ran to the windows.

La Esmeralda is in the Square!

These Parisians come to hear a play and will not listen to it! And what do they mean by this La Esmeralda?

It was dark and cold when Gringoire left the Palace, and he had no place to go. He owed six months rent on his room. He had hoped to pay up with the money from the play—but the play had been a failure! Very well! He would join the Fools at their festival, warm at their fire, perhaps share their feast.

In the Place de Greve, a large crowd was gathered around the fire. Between the crowd and the fire, a young woman was dancing.

She is an angel, a fairy!

Then she turned to a little white goat.

Come, Djali, it is your turn. What month is it?

With his little hoof the goat struck the tambourine   once for the month. Then he told the day and the hour.

Seven times— and the clock strikes seven!

One face in the crowd stared at the dancer harder than any other—a bald man with deep-set eyes. Now he spoke.

There is witchcraft at the bottom of this!

The girl shuddered and turned away. Applause drowned the gloomy words as she began to collect money.

The devil! My pocket's empty.

Now the parade, having gone through the main streets and picked up all the beggars and thieves in Paris, entered the Place de Greve.

Quasimodo was happy. No matter that he was not a real pope, and his people were thieves and murderers. This was the first time people had ever clapped for him.

Suddenly the bald-headed man rushed toward Quasimodo.

It is Dom Frollo, the archdeacon of Notre Dame!

He snatched the golden staff from Quasimodo's hands.

The hunchback leaped down. The crowd feared he would tear the monk to pieces.

Instead, Quasimodo dropped to his knees, and remained so as the priest removed the robe and crown and broke the staff.

Then the priest made a sign to Quasimodo, and they went together, silently, down a dark, narrow street.

It is a wonderful sight! But where shall I find a supper?

Gringoire decided to follow the gypsy girl.

Why not? She must live somewhere. And gypsies are supposed to be very friendly people. . . .

The streets became darker and more empty.

He heard a scream! Turning a corner, he saw her struggling with two men.

Shouting for a guard Gringoire ran forward. One of the men turned upon him.

It is Quasimodo!

Quasimodo struck him once and knocked him down.

Then the hunchback picked up the girl and carried her off. His friend followed.

Suddenly a soldier on horseback came dashing out of the next street, his sword in hand.

He snatched the girl from Quasimodo. Other soldiers held the hunchback, whose friend ran away.

The gypsy turned and looked at the officer.

She thanked the officer, slid to the ground, and ran off.

Gringoire, hurt by his fall, finally came to his senses.

Devil take that hunchbacked monster.

I am freezing! And lost in these crooked streets.

He saw a reddish light down a long, narrow lane.

A fire, God be thanked!

But soon, in the muddy lane, he found himself with strange people.

Cripples—and a blind man!

They came to an open square. One cripple threw down his crutches. The other rose from his cart. The blind man stared Gringoire in the face.

Behold—the Court of Miracles!

Miracles indeed! Blind who see, and cripples who walk and run!

He was in the terrible Cour des Miracles where no honest man dared come; the home of crooks and beggars who faked their injuries.

The area was filled with men, women, children, dogs. The three beggars grabbed Gringoire.

On a barrel near the fire sat the King—the very beggar who had stopped Gringoire's play!

To the King! Lead him to the King!

You have entered our territory. Unless you are a thief, a beggar, or a tramp you must be punished.

Alas, I am not. . . .

Enough! You shall be hanged!

You cannot mean it! I am the poet whose play was given in the Palace today!

Friend, because we were bothered by you this morning, is that any reason you should not be hanged tonight?

They put a crossbar across two poles and hung a rope from it. Gringoire was put on a stool, the rope around his neck.

One moment—I forgot! Before we hang a man, we ask the women if any of them will have him.

Will any among you have this fellow? A husband for nothing! Who'll have one?

No, no . . .he's as lean as a crow.

Hang him, and that will be a pleasure for us all.

Suddenly a bright young girl stepped out of the crowd.

La Esmeralda?

Are you going to hang this man?

Yes, sister—unless you will take him for your husband.

Gringoire felt that he was in a dream.

I will take him.

The noose was removed. Gringoire was lifted from the stool. A clay jug was brought and handed to him.

Drop it on the ground.

Falling, the jug broke into four pieces.

Brother, she is thy wife. Sister, he is thy husband for four years. Go.

In a few moments the poet found himself in a snug, warm room, the husband of this beautiful young woman. He came to her.

Darling Esmeralda!

What do you want with me?

Suddenly she stooped and raised herself again, a little daggar in her hand. The little white goat faced Gringoire with two sharp horns.

What a pair of crazy females! But why did you take me for your husband?

Should I have let you be hanged?

You do not love me—but will you have me for a friend?

Perhaps. I don't even know your name.

At six years of age I was left without my parents. I grew up on the streets with whatever scraps of food were thrown to me.

I tried being a soldier. a monk, a carpenter, a schoolmaster, and I failed. I was fit for nothing, so I became a poet.

One day I met with Dom Frollo, the Archdeacon of Notre Dame, who took a liking to me. To him I owe it that I am a learned man and an author.

Phoebus—what does that mean?

It is a Latin word. It means the sun.

Suddenly the girl and the goat slipped through the door of the next room. Gringoire heard the sound of a lock.

At least she has left me a bed!

Sixteen years earlier, on a day called Quasimodo Sunday, a little creature was laid in the wooden bed on the porch of the church of Notre Dame, where it was a custom to leave orphans and unwanted children in the hope that someone would come along to take care of them.

Is that how they make children nowadays?

'Tis not a child, it's an ape—a monster! It should be drowned . . .or burned!

A young priest had been listening to their talk. Now he came forward and held out his hand over the poor child.

I will take this child.

His heart melted with pity; he took the child in his arms and carried him away.

Didn't I tell you that Monsieur Frollo is a witch?

At that time, Frollo was a priest of Notre Dame. It was there that he baptized this child, who was soon twisting and hopping under the arches of the church.

Notre Dame was his home, his country, his world. He knew and loved every inch of it.

He climbed its towers like something between monkey and mountain goat.

The statues, both saints and monsters, were his friends.

Most of all he loved the bells, even though they had made him deaf.

The one human being whom Quasimodo loved, as much or even more than his cathedral, was Claude Frollo—who had raised him, protected him, taught him, and made him bell ringer.

Although Quasimodo loved him, Frollo was feared by the other boys around the church.

Now let's return to our story. The day after the Festival of Fools, Quasimodo was brought into court.

You are accused of attacking a woman and of fighting the members of the guard. What do you say for yourself?

The deaf prisoner thought that the judge was asking his name.

Quasimodo thought the judge had asked his profession.

Quasimodo.

Are you making fun of me?

Bell ringer at Notre Dame.

Bell ringer! How dare you answer me without respect. I'll make you sorry.

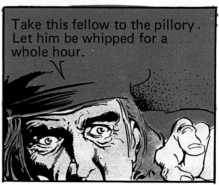

Take this fellow to the pillory. Let him be whipped for a whole hour.

In the Place, where the day before Quasimodo had been cheered as the Pope of Fools, he was now tied on the wheel of the pillory.

As the crowd laughed and cheered, a man climbed the steps to the platform, carrying a whip of long, white tails.

He placed an hourglass on a corner of the pillory. With each turn of the wheel, the whip rose and fell, until the sands had run out, and the hour had passed.

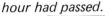

Then the wheel stopped. He still had to remain on the pillory an hour. He opened his eye and glared at the crowd that laughed and threw stones.

At last, breaking his silence, he cried out in a broken voice.

Water!

His cry for help only made the crowd laugh louder.

Drink your water out of this.

Again Quasimodo called; again they laughed more.

Water!

Then the crowd let a young girl pass who came near the pillory.

It was the gypsy girl he had tried to carry off! Thinking she had come to hurt him he shrank away.

Instead she gently lifted a cup to his dry lips.

A big tear trickled down his face. He drank greedily. The crowd cheered as La Esmeralda came down from the pillory.

Hooray!

Hooray!

The time of his whipping having passed, Quasimodo was set free. Two months passed. At a house across from Notre Dame Cathedral, a group of rich young ladies was gathered, together with a handsome young Captain.

It is Dom Frollo, the Archdeacon.

How he looks at the dancing girl!

Let the gypsy beware! He is not fond of gypsies.

Phoebus called to Esmeralda. Shyly she made her way into the house.

Come in, child. Do you remember me?

Oh, yes!

Why did you hurry away that night? Did I scare you?

Oh, no!

A lovely girl, is she not?

But poorly dressed!

Does she run about the streets in that short skirt?

If she covered her arms, they would not be so sunburned!

Come, make your goat act for us. Is it a miracle, or witchcraft?

I don't know what you mean!

If you have no act to show us, you can leave.

So Esmeralda left. After a few moments' thought, Captain Phoebus followed her.

Several evenings later at nightfall, Phoebus and a friend left the tavern where they had been drinking together.

Are you sure the gypsy with the goat will come?

No doubt of it! I meet her at seven o'clock.

Have you any money left? I must have some!

Quiet, friend! I have a song for you.

Then the drunken man sank gently to the ground and began to snore. Nearby in the shadow, a hooded man watched and listened.

Walking on, Phoebus saw a moving shadow behind.

The figure came up and grabbed Phoebus' arm.

You lie!

My ears do not know that word! Draw your sword!

Another time. You forget your meeting.

True! But I must have money, and I haven't a cent.

I will give you money if you hide me in some corner where I may see if the girl is really the one you named.

Thanks! It will make no difference to me!

They went to a house where an old woman opened the door; then showed them upstairs to an attic room.

This way, gentlemen!

This way, sir!

Claude Frollo—for he was the man in the hood—entered, and hid in the dust. His brain seemed on fire.

A few minutes later, a beautiful and graceful Esmeralda came in.

Do not think me bad; I fear what I am doing is wrong —but I love you!

And I love you, my angel, and never loved any other!

She raised her eyes with a look of happiness.

Oh, this is the moment at which one ought to die!

Why die at such a moment? This is the very time to live!

Phoebus, teach me your religion so that we may be married.

Marry? A silly idea! Do people love one another more for a few words spoken by a priest?

The priest's face against the door was like a tiger looking out of its cage. His eyes flashed.

The gypsy's head hung sorrowfully.

Oh, leave me, Captain, I beg you!

I see plainly that you love me not.

Not love you! Would you break my heart? My soul, my life, my all, are yours! I want nothing else!

Phoebus took her into his arms. All at once she saw above the Captain's head, another face—angry, twisted with hate and a hand holding a knife in the air.

Scared to death, she saw the knife come down and rise again. She fainted.

I am lost!

Coming to, she found herself with soldiers all around. The priest was gone.

A month passed. Gringoire and the gypsies were very worried about La Esmeralda, who had not returned. One day Gringoire followed a crowd into the Palace of Justice.

Who are they trying?

A young woman, for murdering a King's officer. They say she's a witch.

An old woman who looked like a bag of rags was being questioned.

. . . .I heard a scream upstairs, and the window open. From my window I saw a man in a black cloak drop to the street.

I was frightened and called the guard. We found the Captain with a dagger in him, and the girl pretending to be dead. A pretty job! It will take me weeks to scrub the floor clean!

Suddenly, to his horror, Gringoire saw La Esmeralda was the girl who was on trial.

Where is Phoebus? For mercy's sake, tell me if he still lives!

Silence! Bring in the second prisoner.

In those days it was common to find animals guilty of witchcraft. Djali was made to perform his tricks.

It is bewitched.

The goat surely has the devil in him.

The president of the court then spoke to La Esmeralda.

Girl, you with the devil's goat, did stab and kill Phoebus de Chateaupers. Do you deny this?

I deny it! It was a priest—a priest who follows me!

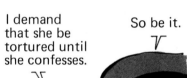

I demand that she be tortured until she confesses.

So be it.

Shaking all over, La Esmeralda was led down a long corridor into a frightening dark cell.

My dear child will you not confess?

No.

In that case, please sit on this bed.

Esmeralda looked wildly around the room, and shook in fright.

What shall we begin with?

The boot.

An ironbound wooden boot was placed around her small foot. A screw was tightened. At that first pain, she screamed.

Wait! Do you confess?

Everything! I confess!

La Esmeralda again entered the court, pale and trembling.

You have confessed, then, all your crimes of magic and of murder?

Whatever you say, only put me to death soon!

She heard a chilling voice pronouce the words.

You shall be drawn in a cart, barefoot, to the Church of Notre Dame, and there confess your sins to a priest; then taken to the Place de Greve and hanged; and your goat likewise.

She was thrown into a dark cell where she stayed in a daze. One day the door creaked on its hinges and a man dressed in black entered.

Are you ready to die? It will be tomorrow.

Why not today? It is a long time till then!

Without light! Without fire! You must be very unhappy.

I want to leave this place! I am cold, I am afraid, and there are things that crawl on me.

Then come with me!

Oh! Who are you?

The man pushed back his hood. It was the priest whose face had followed her for so long! She covered her eyes.

I love you!

Are you afraid of me?

Yes! For months you have followed me! What have I done? Why should you hate me?

Ah! What love!

The love of one who will burn in hell.

Listen! Before I saw you I was happy. But from the day I saw you dancing I was crazy. I followed you, watched you. Each day I loved you more.

I had the idea of carrying you off! We had you in our arms when that officer came up and saved you.

Oh, my Phoebus!

Not that name! Girl, have pity on me! You do not know what unhappiness is! To love a woman—be a priest—to be hated—to see her waste her love on a silly fool!

We could still be happy! I could help you escape. We could find sunshine, blue sky...oh, save yourself! Help me!

What has happened to Phoebus?

He is dead.

Get away, monster! Murderer! Leave me to die! Nothing shall bring us together, not even hell itself!

Silently, slowly, Claude Frollo began to climb the stairs. His face was horrible. Esmeralda fell with her face to the ground.

Phoebus, meanwhile, was not dead. Though badly wounded, he had recovered. He felt that he had been caught in the spell of witchcraft, had been made to look foolish, and was eager to forget the whole business. One fine morning, two months after the stabbing, he came again to call upon the lady who lived opposite Notre Dame.

What a crowd! Look! It's the gypsy with the goat!

I—I don't —what gypsy?

They watched the girl. Suddenly Esmeralda raised her eyes and saw Phoebus.

Phoebus! My Phoebus! You are alive!

Phoebus and the lady quickly went inside, and the window was closed. For Esmeralda, this last shock was too much. She fell to the ground, senseless.

No one had noticed a watcher in the gallery of the church, just above. Suddenly he seized a rope tied to a pillar and glided down.

With one bound he was in the church, holding her over his head.

He struck to the ground the men who held La Esmeralda and carried her off on one arm.

Within the walls of Notre Dame, the prisoner was safe. It was a place of safety. No one could enter and take her away.

Quasimodo held her gently. His eye shed a flood of tenderness upon her. At that moment he was beautiful.

Later in a small room at the top of the church, he brought her food, clothing, and a mattress. She lifted her eyes to thank him, but could not speak.

I frighten you. I am ugly enough, God knows! Do not look at me, but listen!

Stay here during the day. At night you can walk about the church, but do not step out of it, or they will catch and kill you—and it will be the death of me!

Overcome by loneliness, she hid her face. Suddenly something pushed at her knees. She looked down. It was the goat which had escaped and followed her into the church!

The next morning Quasimodo came again. She spoke and he read her lips.

Oh, Djali! I forgot you, but you remembered me!

Why have you saved me?

You have forgotten a man who tried, one night, to carry you off —a man to whom, the next day, you gave water on the pillory! You have forgotten, but he has not.

We have very high towers here. When you wish to be rid of me, tell me to throw myself from the top. You have only to say the word!

He rose, and she made him a sign to stay.

No, no, I must not stay too long. It is out of pity that you do not turn away.

Time passed. Hope filled the girl. Then one day on the roof, she saw Phoebus riding below.

Oh, Phoebus, come! Phoebus, one word!

Phoebus was too far off to hear the call, but the deaf bell ringer understood it.

That is how it is! If only I was handsome on the outside.

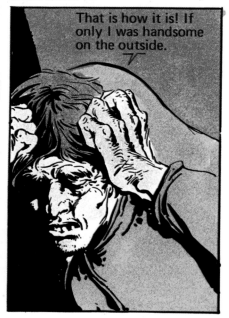

Forcing back tears, he turned to the girl.

Shall I go and get him?

Oh, go! Run! Bring him to me and I will love you!

He hurried down the stairs, but Phoebus had entered the house opposite. Quasimodo waited all day and until late at night before the Captain appeared again.

Come, Captain, a woman is waiting for you—the gypsy who loves you!

Let go of my horse! And tell her that I am going to be married!

Quasimodo returned to Esmeralda. He could not bear to tell her the truth.

I could not find him. Another time I will try again.

Dom Frollo, having heard how Esmeralda had been saved, had shut himself into his cell. For weeks he saw no one. He was terribly upset. At last he went out and found Pierre Gringoire.

How goes it with you, Master Pierre?

Well enough, Master.

What has happened to the gypsy who saved your life?

I'm not sure. I was told that she was safe in Notre Dame.

I can tell you more. The court has passed a special law. In three days' time they will enter the church and seize her.

Then she will be hanged. Will you do something to save her?

Yes, if I do not get hanged myself.

I have it! I will tell the beggars and thieves. She is their favorite. If they attack the church, we can carry her off in the confusion!

Good! We'll do it tomorrow.

The next night, Quasimodo could not sleep. He was uneasy. He locked the great iron bars that closed the church doors. Then he went to the top of the north tower and looked out into the darkness over Paris, keeping guard like a good dog, with a heart full of fear. Suddenly he saw movement below—people—a crowd—pouring into the street before the church.

Then torches were lighted. He could see men and women armed with clubs, sticks, and pickaxes.

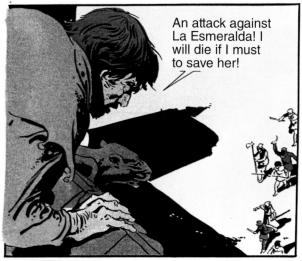

An attack against La Esmeralda! I will die if I must to save her!

Thirty strong men carrying sledgehammers and crowbars made for the great door of the church.

Suddenly with a terrible crash, a great beam fell from the sky, crushing a dozen men!

The crowd ran in every direction, staring up at the sky.

We needed something to knock down the door and the moon has thrown us one! To work, force the door!

The men picked up the beam and smashed it against the great door.

54

A shower of stones began to rain down on the attackers.

Two streams of molten lead fell in a deadly shower.

All eyes were raised. Near the top of the building a flame lighted the statues of devils and dragons—and among the monsters was one that moved from place to place.

The brave hunchback had been lucky. Workmen on the roof had left piles of stones, rolls of lead, great beams with which he had fought the attackers. But now they tried a new method.

A ladder was raised against the church wall and they began to climb.

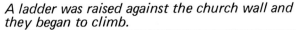

But before they could set foot on the roof, Quasimodo caught hold of the ladder and pushed it from the wall with superhuman force.

But more ladders were found. Soon Quasimodo saw attackers climbing on all sides. He had no way of holding off all these men with angry faces.

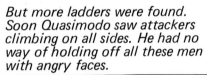

All at once a troop of soldiers on horseback poured into the square like a hurricane!

The mob fought with courage but at last gave way and ran in all directions.

Swiftly as a bird, Quasimodo flew to the little room he had fought for. It was empty!

During the attack Esmeralda had stayed in her room, fearful and praying. Then she heard a footstep.

Oh!

Fear nothing
It is I, Pierre
Gringoire.

Who is that with you?

One of my friends. Your life is in danger again! We have come to save you. Follow us.

They went down through the church and out to the rear of the cathedral. At the river's edge, a rowboat was waiting.

Slowly they crossed the river. The girl watched the unknown man with secret terror.

They reached the shore. Esmeralda stood for a moment frozen with fear. Then she realized that Gringoire and the goat had disappeared and she was alone with the unknown man.

Who are you?

They reached the Place de Greve. In the middle of it stood the gallows. The man raised his hood.

Dom Frollo! Oh! I knew it must be you!

Listen to me! They are looking for you to hang you. I love you and can save you. There is the gallows. Choose between us!

I feel less horror of that than of you!

I love you! Does this claim no pity? It is a torture, night and day. If a man loves a woman, it is not his fault! Will you hate me forever?

A single word of kindness! Only one word—and I will save you.

You are a murderer!

You must die or be mine! It is your choice!

I belong to Phoebus! You are old, you are ugly! Go your way!

Die, then! I go for the sergeants!

There was the sound of weapons and the tramp of horses as the soldiers came.

Hang her now. It is the king's will.

The hangman slipped the cord about the lovely neck of the girl. He then lifted her on his shoulder and began to climb the ladder.

As daylight returned to Paris, Dom Frollo returned to the church and climbed to the tower overlooking the Place de Greve. Quasimodo followed behind him to see what he was looking at.

He saw La Esmeralda carried to the gallows, and the hangman kick away the ladder. And a terrible laugh burst from Claude Frollo.

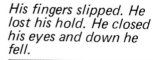

Quasimodo rushed upon him and pushed him into space.

The gutter beneath caught him. He clung to it. Quasimodo did not even look at him.

His fingers slipped. He lost his hold. He closed his eyes and down he fell.

Quasimodo wept. In the square below, the body of the gypsy was joined by the body of the Archdeacon.

There is all I ever loved!

Quasimodo was never seen again. Some two years later, in the tomb where those who had been executed were buried, two skeletons were found. One was a woman and the other, holding her, was a man. His spine was crooked, his head pushed between his shoulders. He had not been hanged. Rather it seemed that he had come there and died.

But Quasimodo had been the soul of Notre Dame. To those who knew he had once existed, Notre Dame appeared empty, dead. The spirit had gone.

The END